Gander's Pond

For Stephen Fry
J. D.

For Ben, who likes rain
H. C.

Text copyright © 1999 by Joyce Dunbar
Illustrations copyright © 1999 by Helen Craig

All rights reserved.

First U.S. edition 1999

Library of Congress Cataloging-in-Publication Data

Dunbar, Joyce.
Gander's pond / written by Joyce Dunbar ; illustrated by Helen Craig.
— 1st U.S. ed.
p.   cm. — (Panda and Gander stories)
Summary: On a hot summer day when Gander wants to make a pond to spla
in, he and Panda finally find a way to catch enough rain water for the proje
ISBN 0-7636-0722-3
[1. Cooperativeness — Fiction. 2. Geese — Fiction. 3. Pandas — Fiction.]
I. Craig, Helen, ill. II. Title. III. Series: Dunbar, Joyce. Panda and Gander sto
PZ7.D8944Gan   1998
[E] — dc21   98-14049

10 9 8 7 6 5 4 3 2 1

Printed in Hong Kong

This book was typeset in AT Arta.
The pictures were done in watercolor and line.

Candlewick Press
2067 Massachusetts Avenue
Cambridge, Massachusetts 02140

Gander's
Pond

Joyce Dunbar

illustrated by

Helen Craig

CANDLEWICK PRESS
CAMBRIDGE, MASSACHUSETTS

The sun was shining.

The day was very dry.

Panda was very thirsty.

Gander was very hot.

"I would like a long, cool drink,"
said Panda.

"And I would like a pond,"
said Gander.

"I am going to make myself a long,
cool drink," said Panda.

"And I am going to make myself
a pond," said Gander.

"How will you do that?"
asked Panda.
"I will wait for it to rain,"
said Gander.
So Panda got himself a long,
cool drink.

Gander waited for it to rain.

He waited . . .

and waited . . .

and waited . . .

until a cloud

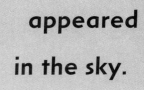

appeared

in the sky.

Big blobs of rain began to fall.

"Now I can make a pond," said Gander.

Gander picked up a bucket and stood in the yard, catching the big blobs of rain.

"It will take a long time to make a pond that way," said Panda.

"You need to run to catch the
rain faster."

"Yes I do," said Gander.

Gander ran around the yard
with his bucket, catching the
big blobs of rain.

But the bucket didn't fill
any faster.

"You need to run faster," said Panda.

"And you need a bigger bucket."

"Yes I do," said Gander.

Gander picked up a bigger bucket

and ran faster around the yard,

catching the big blobs of rain.

But the bigger bucket didn't fill

any faster.

There wasn't nearly enough
for a pond.
"You need a bowl as well,"
said Panda.
"Then you will catch enough
for a pond."
So Gander ran around the yard as
fast as he could with the bigger
bucket and a bowl as well.

Panda ran around with the
small bucket. But there still
wasn't enough for a pond.
"Maybe if we try to catch it
in a tub, then we will have
enough for a pond," said Panda.
"You will have to help me,"
said Gander.

So Panda held one handle on the
tub while Gander held the other.
They caught lots of big blobs
of rain. But there still wasn't
enough for a pond.

"I have an idea," said Panda.

"Why don't we put all our buckets

and bowls out with the tub to

catch the rain?"

"That's a good idea," said Gander.

So they put all their buckets and

bowls out with the tub to

catch the rain.

But the rain slowed down
to a drizzle.

"Oh, dear," said Gander.

"We need to put out all our pots and
pans and buckets and bowls and the
tub. Then we might have enough
water for a pond," said Panda.

"That's a good idea," said Gander.
And they put out all their pots
and pans with their buckets and
bowls and the tub, but the rain
stopped altogether.
"I give up," said Panda.
"So do I," said Gander.

"Let's have a cookie instead,"
said Panda.

So Panda and Gander each ate
a cookie instead.
While they were eating
their cookies, big blobs of
rain began to fall again.

They got bigger and . . .

bigger and bigger!

They fell faster and . . .

faster and faster!

Suddenly the rain stopped again.

"Look, the buckets are full,"

said Panda.

"So are the bowls," said Gander.

"So are the pots and pans,"

said Panda.

"But the tub isn't full," said Gander.
"If we pour all the water together,
we will have enough for a pond."

So they poured all the water
into the tub.
"Rub-a-dub-dub, a pond in a tub!"
said Gander.

Then Panda had another long, cool

drink while Gander made

a great big splash!